MONEY IS AS INNOCENT AS THE GUN

G Winde

Printed by Lightning Source in the UK.

Lightning Source has received Chain of Custody (CoC) certification from:

- The Forest Stewardship Council™ (FSC®)
- Programme for the Endorsement of Forest Certification™ (PEFC™)
- The Sustainable Forestry Initiative® (SFI®).

Chain of Custody (CoC) is an accounting system that tracks wood fiber through the different stages of production: from the forest, to the mill, to the paper, to the printer and ultimately to the finished book. For publishers, and ultimately consumers, CoC ensures the integrity of the paper supply chain and that the paper used in Lightning Source® printed books are from responsibly managed forests.

Published in 2018 with IngramSpark

ISBN 978-1-7392325-0-4

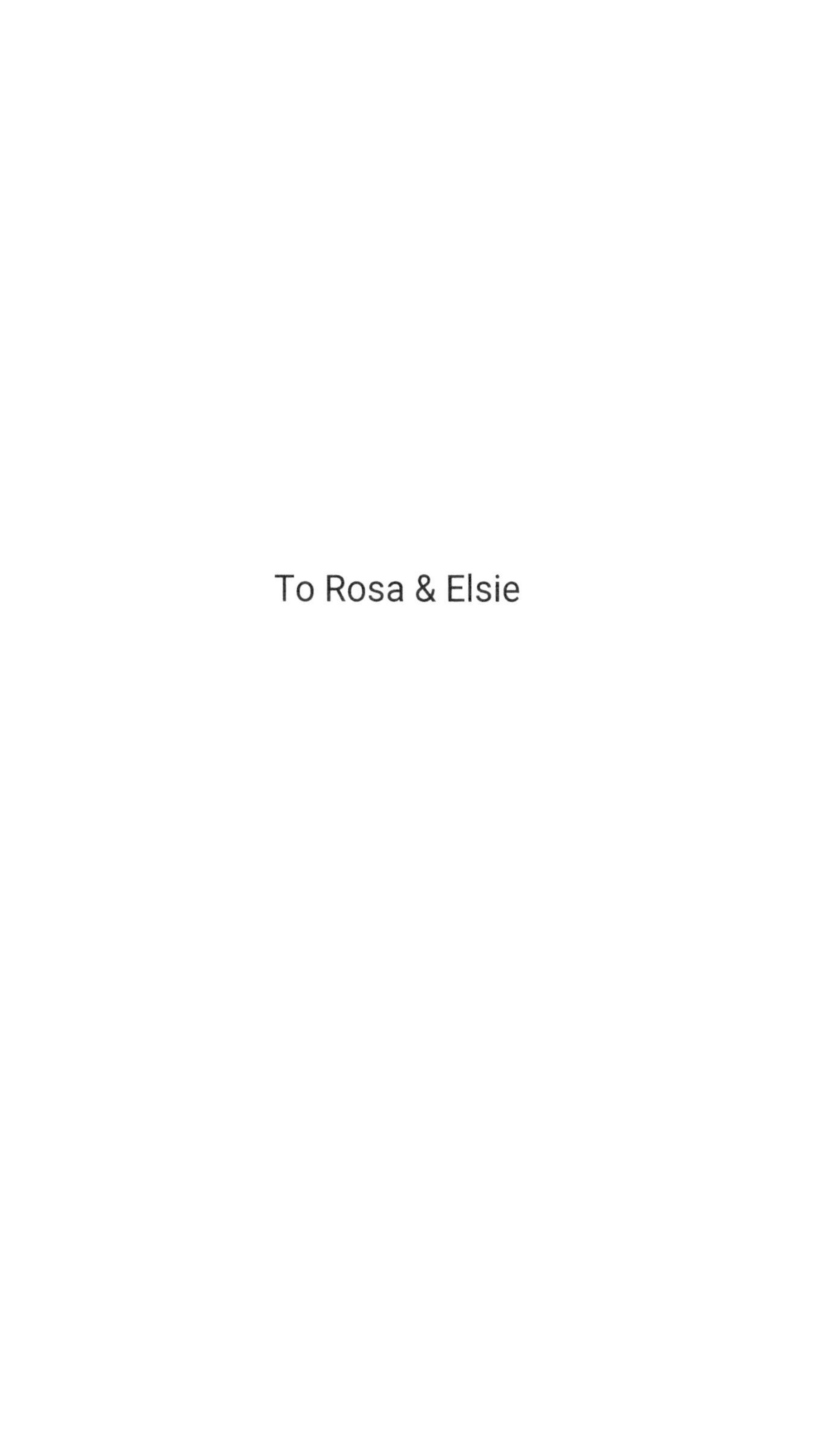

To Rosa & Elsie

Contents

MONEY IS
AS
INNOCENT
AS
THE GUN

Money is as Innocent as the Gun

part 1

Sucking through last straws, sitting behind locked doors; is it the sucking or what we suck up that gives us such, pause?

This story begins with sitting in a job centre, behind sliding doors, there is sucking, there is pause... and last straws.

The claimant was sat in a chair, sat in a chair, in a state, feeling stateless, with a past, now, back-date-less, feeling fat and looking weightless, but the claimant was not weightless, no, she wasn't sat in a chair; not 'in' a chair, like you couldn't see that she was there, this is not a story meant to disturb, to unnerve or to scare, to boggyfie those on Benefits, no; there, in front of the desk in the centre of the job centre, the claimant sits, and shits, herself naked, to the invisible eye; that can see right through her, the Job seeking adviser, you and I. The invisible eye? No? Ok. There the claimant sits, and shits, herself visible, to the naked eye, that belongs to the job seeking adviser, to you and I. 'Now, hold on, hold on', you maybe thinking, 'what about those other tax paying naked eyes that are blinking, for an opportunity, for some scrutiny, of those jobless job seekers seeking to carry out their duty'. Duty? Now there is a beauty. Well, there is the open plan office job centre designs, with their most accommodating windows without blinds, so this and other such scenes can be seen from the street. Whilst taking a leisurely lunch time stroll to the sandwich shop for to eat.

"Mm...so much choice and so little time, erm!, some singed avocado, please, with burnt garroted goats cheese, and some of that shredded Chinese peasant's eye lid, just a drizzle of Bangladeshi textile worker's saliva... on Israeli Apartheid Soda Stream bread." And if your local council have done what this government said, they should do, with that central grant, there should be benches by those windows for you, to sit and view, while sipping your strictly ballroom latte, smooth turn take away?'

Now, before we go through these sliding doors on this venture, into this job centre. Please, when we are there, try not to be wound up when you see, there is the odd privacy, screen, everything can be seen, they can easily be got round and they don't conceal a sound.

One last thing; before setting off on such an expedition, you would be advised, to make something of an exhibition, of your employment situation, your work status; an ID badge, or dress with a certain professional haughty sartorialness, just to assist the security guards in making their decision, who to pepper spray and to escort from the premises, or not; if by any chance, once you've had your lot, you fall into a news paper print rage and a claimant you engage, in physical or verbal abuse, while waving around a copy of the daily noose.

But, rest assured, it's for the staff and public safety, the services of those guards have been secured. G4S, no less...

So, here we are close to the centre of the job centre, lets find a seat, and for the sake of this tale please try to be discrete.

Sat in a chair, in front of the desk in the centre of the job centre; the claimants words were sticking to the back of her throat. Now, please don't let this get your goat. This is not a deliberate lack of cooperation. Please, put that scalpel down, she does not need an operation.

A mime... 'Ah! the 'ace of wands' oh .. mm .. you will be entering a period of abundance, realise that chance is just a state of mind, risk will be abolished and you will have the Midas touch.'

These weren't the words sticking to the back of the claimant's throat, by the way. No, they were still circling for some where to land inside her head. The shape of those words, were the shape of the tread, of the wheels turning in her head.

Sitting in a chair, behind the desk in the centre of the job centre, the Job Seeking Adviser, Ms Gleason, addressed the claimant with five inquiring yes's; is that how many its going to take to loosen these words from the back of the claimant's throat? I wonder. The resemblance these yes's had to the sound that a dog might make when locked in a car parked in direct sun light, increased with each utterance.

I won't do the yes's; because apparently I don't do very good animal impersonations. I will of course - if you insist... Ok!. By the way dogs can't cope with heat, because they've only got sweat glands on their little noses and on the pads of their feet.

'Huh huh huh huh, Yes'.

Looking at these women sat at this desk, in the centre of the job centre, you wouldn't think looking at her; 'now, there is a women with a strong will to live'. No, well, its not necessary, it's not required. She is finding each day waiting for her, there, standing over her as she wakes in the morning, accompanying her, observing her, as it passes; and then standing side by side with the next day; and both of them standing over her as she undresses her eyes to sleep she can feel them both there waiting to begin and to end, to end and begin to begin and to end, to end and to begin, to begin and to end, to end and to begin, to begin and to end, to end and to begin, to begin and to end, to end and to begin.

Looking at this women sat there... if by any chance, you had seen this women before, when she was otherwise engaged, busy not knowing she was born; you might look at her sat there and think, 'well, she knows now'. She'd received a letter about 9, 10 months ago. Not telling her she'd been born. No, that would be a peculiar letter to receive from the Department of Work and Pensions. No, this letter informed her, you have been found capable of work. Found, capable, and in working order. This discovery was made by a business that goes by the name of Atos, whose services this, your, her majesty's government had engaged in an attempt to curb the excesses of those scurrilous, self serving, speculators, GP's? and in her case a CPN, a Community Psychiatric Nurse, too.

'Huh huh huh huh, Yes'...

She arrived far too early to the sports centre that day, that's where the Atos assessments were taking place by the way, She couldn't really afford a taxi, but she couldn't afford to be late, she couldn't afford to get her self into an agitated state, she could afford to leave it in the hands of fate. If by any chance previous medical opinions turn out to be awry, so what, so be it, she wasn't work shy; Work! Work! Work!, she had almost made the ultimate sacrifice for this, your her, majesty's governments nation; she answered the Atos examiner's questions without a drop of hesitation, like a full and frank declaration, doing not a bad impersonation, of her CPN.

I won't do an impersonation of her doing an impersonation of her CPN because, apparently, I don't do very good impersonations of people with PTSD doing impersonations of CPN's. I will of course if you insist... OK?!. Ok...

'It is only through the corners of a past encrusted eyes that she can see the present'.

The expression on the Atos examiners face turned a tad unpleasant, at this most informative, pretense; darkened still further by her insistence, that her star sign being Cancer was not just a coincidence. 'Between 60 and 65 percent of her time, when indoors, is spent sitting or standing with her back nestled against walls; and when mobilising it is necessary, to avoid anxiety, that she sidle along walls through rooms and corridors.'

The Atos examiner refused to accept this had any connection with her being born at noon, between the 21st of June and the 22nd of July. She rained in her thoughts and let out a sigh.

'Huh huh huh huh, Yes'...

So, she was punctual and very well presented, but awarded two points with a click of the mouse when trying to fasten the harness attached to the hoist, she relented. The hoist? The hydraulic hoist by the side of the swimming pool. She was maintaining her dignity but was on the edge of loosing her cool. As you can imagine, its very frustrating trying to fasten fiddly little clasps and buckles with a claw. She'd sacrificed this touch in what we euphemistically called a war. In the line of duty, drawn by her majesty's governments experiments in alchemy, heat devoured her touch, a heat that gave teeth to light, an ingesting light, that devoured what was there before the stars and the planets and a touch and a touch and a touch...

Hoisted up and over the deep end, once the harness was secured; given the comforting words, 'Don't worry we are insured'. She was lowered into the water with the drone of the hydraulic hoist ringing in her ears, she was having problems holding on to tears, that were pricking at the back of her eyes; Chlorine? No, not necessary, not required.

Instructed to, 'unfasten the harness please'. She did, she could, and the previous two points were taken a way with a clickful ease.

With beaded bubbles dreaming from her nose and mouth she sank slowly to the bottom of the pool. So, she was fit for work! Two Atos attendants got her out of the water with a well drilled extrication, one had to apply mouth to mouth resuscitation, whilst her colleague sat and watched with a morbid fascination. Now, you maybe wondering, if mouth to mouth resuscitation was required, what does it take for the imagination to be fired, into following, that it was because of the inhaling and swallowing, of water that she sank, but such a conclusion would not have another body in money's bank, to be withdrawn or not, at money's will, supply and demand, a slight of hand, a trick of the human traffic light spill? Human trafficking is a crime? But, not all the time.

Well, the Atos examiners report made no mention of mouth to mouth resuscitation occurring at all; and her recollection of receiving the 'kiss of life', manifested itself in a feeling of gratitude, deep. Slicing off the top of her dignity, creating a draft, a tiresome fatiguing draft. She didn't have it in writing yet, but she had been found.

'Huh huh huh huh, Yes!'...

Still sat in a chair, in front of the desk in the centre of the job centre, the claimant paused there, she became aware, of a warmth still there, in the partly upholstered chair, where, the previous claimant; who was just about to walk through the sliding doors out of the building, had sat and signed a piece of paper there, on the desk, a pledge, on the desk in the centre of the job centre; that would allow him to use 256 kilowatts of gas, 108 kilowatts of electricity, the use and disposal of 203 gallons of water. To clean and feed himself for the next two weeks. Well, not really, not properly. He also, had credit card payments to meet, and considerable arrears with the water company. He may have been off school on the day that lesson was taught on how to spot a boy or girl who was likely to develop a dependency on alcohol and should not and could not be trusted with water, Water?... money. And he was putting aside £3 a week, every week, toward getting a pair of shoes that didn't leak; well, when you haven't kissed or caressed, in over 18 months, there can be hope in not making a squeak, squeak, squeak... Now please don't look so concerned, that claimant leaving the building, hadn't just signed that piece of paper, its ok, he'd been given permission, ok?. He'd shown Ms. Gleason evidence of job applications he had made, interviews he had attended, proof of phone calls and e mails requesting further job applications. As far as she was concerned he had fulfilled his job seekers agreement for the previous 2 weeks; ok? Ok?

'Huh huh huh huh!, Yes!...'

The claimant reached into her coat pocket and took out a piece of paper and unfolded it on her lap. She began to gag in a juddering rhythm, loosening the words from the back of her throat, well all except five. The words fell on to the paper. Now, during this attempt by the claimant to loosen the words from the back of her throat, the resemblance the movement of the claimant's tongue had, to a dogs tail wagging, that had just been let out of a car parked in direct sunlight, increased with each word. She put the piece of paper on the desk, and in the middle of this paper on the desk in the centre of the job centre were the words; 'I have lost my entire fortnights job seekers allowance on a horse in the 3.45 at Kempton, and I need the money replacing, please'.

Ms. Gleason didn't respond immediately, appearing not to understand this note, giving the appearance of not understanding, she gestured to the claimant with a nod, that they peruse this 'document' together. The claimant leaned over the desk and she gripped the claimant's neck, holding her there she leaned in, the warmth of her breath touched the claimant's ear as she opened her mouth to speak. But, there was nothing to say, it had already been said, this claimant had been sacrificed, escape goat spit filled her head.

Now there is a difficult substance for wheels to turn in, no matter what the tread. This grip had loosened the last five words from the back of the claimant's throat and they were now trying to get out of her mouth. The grip released, the claimant slumped back into the chair. 'I haven't eaten for three days', scuttled out between the claimants lips. 'I-haven't-eaten-for-three-days', oh... that's six words. By the way the claimant hadn't just given her that bit of information about her diet, no, the claimant had presented it to her in a manner that might provoke feelings of pity. The claimant didn't intend them to come out that way, the claimant didn't intend to share that bit of information with her at all. Still sat in a chair, behind the desk in the centre of the job centre, the possible consequences of what she had just done to the claimant was sinking into the lining of her stomach, her mouth dried. She pushed the button under the desk!? Arjan, who was standing by the sliding doors, got a message in his ear piece. With extendable baton and pepper spray concealed, he set off at a purposeful stroll along the carpeted aisles towards desk five. Was this going to come down to her word against hers?

As Arjan rounded the 'privacy screen', she gestured for him to wait. Appearing to be in some kind of state of denial she was engaging the claimant – she could see the bruises forming on the claimant's neck – engaging the claimant in familiar conversation. "Oh?, So, what was the name of this horse?". The claimant, despite Arjan's presence, leaned over the desk; the warmth of the claimant's breath touch her ear as the claimant opened her mouth to speak, "Too big to fail" the claimant replied. "'Too big to fail'. It fell at the fifth or was it the sixth". Tears were pricking at the back of her eyes. Pepper spray? No. not necessary, not required.

She recognised this; feeling, and if she wasn't mistaken, all she'd have to do was... she wasn't going to have to do anything, she was just going to get up off the chair and leave the building. She stood up, pushed the chair back, sidled along the edges of the carpeted aisles, out through the sliding doors and into the streets.

Arjan, looked over at the claimant sat in a chair in front of the desk in the centre of the job centre. The claimant lifted the collar of her coat, to conceal the marks on her neck, where Ms. Gleason's claw had gripped her. She stood up, pushed the chair back, walked along the carpeted aisles and followed Ms Gleason through the sliding doors. The Spark of love and solidarity can occur in the strangest of moments.

part 2

I would like to ask for some audience participation, at this point, if I may, ok? Please join me thinking about money ....

No matter how much thought we give money,

Nothing is bought, but worry,

It has a short, and defensive fuse, money's muse,

My meditations on money it will so often just refuse,

I really don't understand what it's got to loose, money,

And why its muse should get so funny,

When I'm just searching for money's inspiration,

It's as if I'm making some kind of allegation,

I wouldn't be surprised if at the end of this journey, into money,

We don't find a tubby bald North American actor sitting sweating in the dark, saying,

"oh the worry, the worry".

All money appearing in this work is fictitious,

Any resemblance to real money, dead or alive is purely coincidental,
I've had to insert that or money's muse was gonna go fundamental,

Thinking about money, a synonym for worry?
an inspiration to bury, My head in the sand,
Because, since giving up the day job to do this,
things have got a bit out of hand,
It appears that dreams only come true if they make money,
and money only comes true if it makes dreams,
Now there is a vicious circle, in which hopes become money's schemes,

So, I got some sand to go in a bucket the other day,
And I know realistically, it won't keep the debt collectors at bay,
But, when my head is in side, I can't hear a sound,
though, as of yet no relief has been found,
cause i can hear some one thinking, and its me, and its about money,

So, I was thinking about money,
And it might just be me, but, may be its a forgery; minted?
Have you ever heard, such a smoke screen of a
word, for something that's just printed?
and if money is just printed, just a print!
then deep down, deep down we're all skint.
Skinflint skint; skint, the past participial of to skin, money thin skin,
Circulation skin thin, imagination-thin skin,
with limitless degrees of sep-ar-a...

Oh, maybe I shouldn't be expressing such thoughts in a public place,
I could end up in the courts, with charges to face, of treason,
for even suggesting there's a reason, to believe that legal tender,
is just a poisonous printed paper pretender,
Yes, sorry, I've clearly misunderstood the situation;
it's a magical ritual incantation, minting,
not just a copying, not just a printing,
and we are all under its spell,
day after day in this rising whirl pool of a wishing well,
of buy, borrow, sell, buy borrow sell, buy borrow sell,
and please don't think that I would dream of making any comparison
between the picture of Dorian Gray,
and the power of money expanding with each circulating dream day,
and its origin, now its servant, with nothing to say,
in a state of servile paralysis,
In need of some kind of community analysis,
we have nothing to say, just buy, borrow, sell, pay,

Pay, pay, that's an interesting word to say, mm, Pay,
it smacks of obey,
to pay and pay and pay until our dying...
If death is a penalty, are we really living or just parking?
And is life the fine to pay?

Pay, pay! a bit of a kinky word to say, pay,
Not the sort of word you want to use with to much conviction,
It could result in some inappropriate friction,

Pay, just pay, just payments, just Wars,
our imagination's sores,
to those financial action scenes Hollywood adores,
The only way to stop a bad man with money,
is a good man with money,
money chasing money down narrowing corridors,
into merchant diced stores,
its good money fighting bad money for money's cause,
I know that its often said that with a big lie,
That it's not visible just to the naked eye?
But... Banks and their governments, a long and elaborate con?,
Surely, they're not dissimilar to the religious one,
except, gods are in stories we told,
and money is telling our story in continuous unfold,

While money makes money we are awash with coincidence,
money is not worth the paper it's printed on, ups!,
Is that a bit strong?,
Ok, money is worth more than the paper it's printed on,
wait a minute that sounds like a con,
OK, so money is worth more and less than the paper its printed on,
Hold on, is that a contradiction,
but, money is worth more and less than the papers it's printed on,

How can what something is worth,
be more and less than what it is?,

by the way this isn't a quiz,
though I must ask,
when and where did we decide what is worth money?
Oh, sorry I think I've got that the wrong way round,
that does sound a bit funny,
when and where did we decide what is worth money, or not?
We haven't left that up to those who've got,
so much more than a lot?
Those who are trying to write our plot;
I think not,
cause when you've got, that kind of money,
its really got you, and when you haven't got money,
it's really got you then!,
so where and when,
did we decide what is worth money or not,
I'm assuming that decision was not made on the basis of what we have or haven't got,
I think I'm talking about the sub plot,

the real we,
the substance of what we like to think of as the basis of democracy,
Oh dear, have we left it up to money to decide for itself what it is or isn't worth?
how are we going to explain that to our children and our children's children?
here's an idea, Tell them, "money not of this earth",

"But, how did it get here?
In some meteor shower, discovered by monks in an ivory tower"?
and where did it come from?
the Sun?

personified and instituted, the original Science Fiction,
maybe that's at the heart of this contradiction,
the Royal refrain and its religion,
in a coalition with the banks and their governments domain, circulated
a calculated faith of measured mystery,
And the banks took a slash, and money made
a splash, on the stage of history,
a golden shower mouth agog, steaming fog, of class war,
and money's old friend the judiciary,
amended, nay, repealed the Christian law,
on crucifixion,

though, the industrial revolution according to science fiction,
was a mass alien conscription,
evidence suggests it was more like a genocidal crucifixion,
though we were like an alien race,
with the new machine face,
that did not know our place,
we were treated worse than cattle,
worked to the bone until the, oh so premature death rattle,
men, women, children together in toil,

worked till the blood began to boil,
and serum builds up in the perineum sack,
just like the Christian saviours heart attack,
and a transubstantiation, of almost an entire population;
and money rose on the 3rd day,
and we were free, to work for money, and to pray pay,
pray pay, pray, pay, pray, pay, pray, pay, pray...

When money makes money it doesn't give a toss with coincidence

Money couldn't have got off the ground
though, with us still working for free,
serfdom had to be abolished along with slavery,
Cos, who'd have bought what we had made,
if we hadn't been paid,
for the pleasure,
of turning this earth into money's treasure,
But now, those wooden racks and nails are exported to warmer climbs,

I am waiting for the United Nations to define Class War Crimes?
They call them accidents but they're more like repeated episodes of money's old times,
Money begs questions with see saw sighs,
of empty cradle rocking eyes,
Beseeching answers from silent air, carbonised good byes,
Bargains to take the breath away!

So, now what we earn, is of little concern, its buy the by,
cos there is to borrow and to borrow and to borrow...
and all our yesterdays could have lit us to another age,
if the credit card and the mortgage,
had been the rage, before 1833, they...
they might not have abolished slavery,
they might have expanded it on the grounds of discrimination,
to include the 99 percent of the nation,

When money makes money it doesn't give a toss with coincidence,
It's the siren on the rocks you see, money,
it came as a shock to me, money
that it put the mock in de-moc-racy, money
but, now I understand what they mean by liquidity,
taking the piss, money
the theory and the practice, money
speculation, speculator, money
the genuine minted ballot paper, money
whose voting hand, we in frustration,
try to hold and shake with such adulation,
creating slap sick scenes of capitulation,
and frowns of futility, with shrugs of incredulity,
because it's only by chance that you can hold
and shake that which has no visibility,
yet has a grip like drying cement,

when hand in glove with government,
Money begs questions in a homeless hand, that
when closed, can feel the speculated interest rate shifting sand,
that buried the long life security planned, and
now refuses to even try to hold the invisible hand,
It has its own speculations canned,

When money makes money, we are awash with canned incidence,

The Royal refrain and its religion,
now eclipsed by the banks and their governments domain,
no trumpets heralded in this money reign,
but a busy imperial concrete abstraction of limitless gain,
concrete abstraction?, concrete abstraction?,
the abstract made concrete?
What a feet, of clay, on a sacred golden statue say?

Concrete abstraction?
is that some kind of sophisticated distraction,
That provokes no reaction, because the abstract made concrete,
the concrete made abstract is just a fact, of life, of living,
So all we create and all we make is beyond the giving,
beyond the receiving,
As long as we keep on believing, in this abstract construct,
in which 99 percent of us are fucked,
hooked, on this hook of gobbledygook,

which we have mistook,
for worth,
worth? the most flexible software on earth?

money is worth, in a money state,
It's as if the hands of fate have been de-skilled,
a self fulfilling prophecy being perpetually fulfilled,
worth is money and money is worth,
its like all the gods we've ever imagined have come down to earth,
and now we really are barb mired in chance,
hooked, hard wired to dance,
to the money siren song,
are we hard wired to dance to money's siren song
while we suck-a-long-a-life-time through last straws, that give us such...

'I'm not putting up with this any more. I am gonna put a brick through a banks window...' 'Pause',
'I am going to hack into the computer systems of banks and share out those numbers...', 'Pause',
'I am gonna to get together with my friends and work mates and organise and were gonna occupy money... what?. Occupy money?'
'Pause'.

Government by possession of the people's fear for their possessions,
in spiraling repossessions, of re-occurring recessions,
'Father?' 'Yes', 'What did you do during the Great Recession?'
'Oh, I did rather well, yes I did very well'

'Dad, Dad, wake up, Dad!'
Recessions; there are no such things as recessions,
there are just callous calculated concessions,
made by governments to those who would take and make possessions,
of us and what is ours,
the foundations of all those sky scraping towers,
recessions? Huh! money doesn't want to learn lessons,
money doesn't need to learn lessons,

Money is... more... 'drum roll'... or... 'less... money!' more or less...
more or less, more or less...
The more money there is, the more every thing is worth,
but, the more money there is, the less money is,
cos, the less the numbers are worth,
but, the more everything is worth,
The less money there is,
now you might want to brace yourselves for this,
the less money there is, the less every thing is worth,
but, the less money there is, the more money is, cause the more the numbers are worth,
is it of this earth!?

Demand and Supply? Is that a lie, a trick of money's light, an illusion,
a dubious conclusion,
based on the notion that money's circulation is our motion,
for the sake of some alien spaceship's accumulation?,

'Have you noticed the designs of skyscrapers are becoming more aerodynamic?'

Supply and demand is that some kind of extraterrestrial slight of hand?
The more there is of something the more it is worth,
the more there is to go around,
more needs and desires can be explored and found,
the less there is of something, the more it's worth,
Is that a perspective from on this earth,
or just the less we are worth?,

Money is just numbers, more or less; more money, more numbers,
less money, less numbers... less numbers?,
money less numbers!? Money numberless!!...
Money numberless, that would be a broken spell on earth,
Everything would be worth less, price less,
worth less, price less, worth less,
worthless, priceless, priceless, worthless,
You say worthless, I say priceless,
Lets call the whole thing... the whole thing,
the whole thing the whole thing?,
the whole thing the whole thing!?
The whole thing the...?

Oh! GDP, as simple as ABC, as easy as 123, ABC, GDP, Doh-rae-me,
GDP, Gross Domestic Product, a measurement of out put in a particular place;

the in put?...ah... I can't... quite put a name to that....
You?, you, you, you, you, the subversive 'we',
the hidden collectivity,
the 'we' that dare not speak it's name,
in this divisive, hidden money game,

as I said, it came as a shock-to-me, money
That it put the mock in de-moc-racy, money
but thinking about it, this is more like some kind of the-hoc-racy,
where money debt is now the sin,
without origin, that we are born in,
a transition of transgression did transpire,
the shadow of the skyscraper, shaped like a spire?,
towers of power, powers for debt,
spiraling to nowhere, never to be met,
no longer the source of original sin,
this, oh so weak and wicked fleshful skin,
which now you can buy shares in,

My flesh is weak, but not as weak as my credit rating,
Mm...which makes it a bit difficult Internet dating,
F.U.C.K, so, yesterday,
F.U.C.C, me,
For Unlawful Carnal Knowledge, becomes, For Unpaid Credit Card,
you just have to pronounce that last C, a little bit hard!,

no longer clergy's sermons are required to be ringing in our ears,
there are much more profitable insecurities and fears,
for us to realise, through Scripture of the advertise,

Money begs questions with an empty stomach blurred concentration, of
the child's attempted separation
of the words from the page, with
a self fulfilling whispered rage,
behind the scenes of inadequacies stage, oh,
but that the words could draw more than tears, on to the page,
and that child could walk on to that stage,
and with eloquence make real that rage,

Money begs questions like it hasn't eaten all day, I'll
do my impersonation of money begging questions if I may,
Money begging questions, one of the most difficult mimes in the book, so
often mistaken for being forsaken, whilst being mistook,
being mistook whilst being forsaken, should not
be mistaken, for being lost whilst... orally taken!?,
"oh father, why hast thou for-suck me", is a biblical loss in translation,
the clergy should have been given clear and unequivocal clarification,

but trust in banks and in any church? no, no,
Neither has a conscience to search,
they both live and breath by the same spirit,
an abstraction with out limit,

eternal credit line,
faith and numbers combine,
cloud nine financial instrument design,
and another miraculous transubstantiation,
without a shred of a shroud of fabrication,
through the credit default swap incantation,
derivative sin without origin,
spinning investing vested veil,
and now our debts like our sins are up for sale,

spend and ascend, spend and descend, spend and transcend,
Spend and offend, spend and amend, 'does that look any smaller,
bigger, smaller, bigger... spend and re-offend,
spend and condescend,
spend and ascend!,
spend and descend!,
spend and ascend!,
Spend, spend spend spend spend spend spend spend spend
spend spend spend, spend spend spend... skint!!,

skint; the past participial of to skin,
money thin skin, circulation thin skin,
imaginations thin skin, with limitless degrees of separation,
Is debt what we are bandaged in, bondage,
bandaged, bondage, bandaged!, bondage!, bandaged!, bondage!, bandaged...

you say bondage I say bandage, lets call the whole thing...
'a kinky first aid hostage situation' ..
what? .. 'a kinky first aid hostage situation?'
99 percent of every nation,
in a kinky first aid hostage situation?

Sorry, sorry, I think I am suffering from sham shock; sham shock?
it's a condition you get when you've been lied to a lot,
it's very common in a sham-shoc-racy,
of a de-moc-racy, that's more like a the-hoc-racy,
where money debt is now the sin against the churches of money?,

Which is Topsy turvy and not funny,
cos if money,
the manifestation of this imaginary spirit,
which the banks and their governments have without limit,
then where is the time and place
for the source of all grace, the human spirit,
that exists and thrives when what's yours is mine,
and mine is yours, and flowers in the beauty of a common cause,

let's unhinge money's doors,
and make those scary towers of scary powers, ours,
Let's disobey... that's so easy to say... let us disobey,
those pretend sins of pretend debts we don't actually have to pay,
Let us disobey,
Let's pauper faith and beggar belief,
and make our own relief,

from this money thief,
this Money State,
that flies the self interest rate,
higher than a kite,
where the real unwritten right, to life and liberty,
is money makes you… free, money makes you… free?

money fakes us free,
cause, if freedom is meant to be ours,
not something circulated after a ransom has
been paid to those golden showered
powered towers?
Then, freedom would be found, lived and loved
in the weaving fabric of our interaction,

not the grip of some numbered expansion,
or contraction, in reaction,
to the movement of a fraction, of a percent,
cause that makes us still a frightened animal,
except this time we don't even know we've got a scent.
"You fill up my senses, like a man in a forest… "

Is it a contradiction for freedom to have a fate?,
not in a Money State,
A Money State is a criminal caper, the
difference between a money state and a police state;
after the scary knock on the door in a police state, they

take you away, for something you might say.
After the scary knock on the door in a money state, you
lose your home, your family, they take your belonging away,
for something you couldn't pay,

A Money State is a criminal caper,
and the smoke screen is the ballot paper,
Cos, this periodic ability vote
is just a variation on the sacrificial goat,
except the trick this time, is we are meant to
be the gods to appease, please!
democracy; to money, is similar to a disease,

the further freedom is pulled away,
from the ability to pay,
there lurking in the shadows is freedom's doomsday,
if the symptoms of democracy ever come anywhere close to,
"red – a world about to dawn, black...",
democracy will find itself like an unwanted puppy in a river in a sack,

When money makes money there can be such a boss with coincidence

Money made Hitler and his like,
not just their fear and loathing of the Disabled, Trade Unionists,
Homosexuals, Travelers, Gypsies, Socialists, Jews,
Money had the right to and it did choose,
Hate can't fund an election campaign,
Money did, and money will, no matter how cruel, inhuman and insane,

and do you think money's changed?
Well, it looks and tastes pretty much the same to me,
and it doesn't give an F.U.C.C, about the practice of de-moc-racy,

When money makes money we can be the dross with coincidence.

Poetry treats money like a bad smell,
'nothing rhymes here, there's nothing to tell',
money treats poetry, in a nut shell, in a nut shell,
just ripples on a wishing well,
experiments are being carried out,
on this universal equivalent known as cash,
scientists are circulating it's particles at high
speed and letting them crash,

and in the core of the aftermath of this collision,
there is an interesting vision,
'anti-money is real',
it's qualities, something you can touch,
something you can judge, and something you can feel,
Now, the banks and their governments, are
more than a little concerned about these experiments,
because it turns out, under the microscope, the
majority of anti-money, is made up of matter,
and energy and some other stuff, and
there is enough,

to clothe, to feed, to house and to educate every
man, women and child on this earth,
enough as enough, not some comparative equivalent worth,

Now I know anti-money sounds funny,
but, to us unscientific folk
Gravity was just a joke, until we learned how to fly!,

When money makes money we are awash with coincidence,

Maybe this game of equivalence,
is going to have to be redefined,
because it turns out the earth does mind,
the equivalent becoming the real,
because then the earth is just the notional part of any deal.
A flood damaged bargain basement fire sale steal,

And the real is?... and the deal is?
Our equivalent fueled actions,
are not even fractions,
of a percentage of numbers on a screen,
regurgitating abstraction,
over and over for the sake of extraction,
of more to the power of more.
What is money for... Who is money for?

'Hold on, hold on...' I hear you say
'...what's so ambivalent about this universal equivalent?

Surely it is just a means of exchange,
it's nothing to estrange, us,
just... a way to rearrange, us.'
and the history, of rearrangement through this convention,
to numerous to mention,
has given it more than a bad name,

But what can you expect, without conscience,
without honour without shame?
And still there is the poor to try, and to blame.
There's a crisis in the brand, money,
off shore and on land, honey,
So; to the re-branding, of
this universal equivalent of not such long standing,
There'd be an opening ceremony of course, that
goes with out saying
the televised depiction of the history of our paying,

Paying for everything that's always already been ours,...
shh... is that the sound of more showers?
filling this whirl pool of a wishing well,
with lullaby, borrow, sell,
lull and buy, borrow, sell,

There is a dictatorship of accumulation; to be overcome?,
with an ideology that the parts do equal the sum,
Maybe this, their 'money' is the last dark art,

of creating the illusion of keeping us together,
while keeping us apart,

'Hold on hold on', I hear you say,
'... surely we are all under money's spell,
in this circulating lullaby of a wishing well,
together, day after day,'

Mm, but the sum of us are more lulled than lulling,
more spun against than spinning,
Banks and their governments are like churches creating sin,
for their sinning,
99 percent to be almost precise,
at the mercy of this loaded money dice,
with a price,
on our 'heads or tails?
counterfeit spliced behind money's veils,
has money made us the forgery?,
humanity, a case of mistaken,
misshapen, identity,?

When money makes money, we are the loss with coincidence,

and our absence is yours and your absence is ours,
lets dismantle these hostage taking,
dictating towers,
of golden showering powers,

Money is as Innocent as the Gun

Money, is just numbers, for
our waking slumbers,
to repeat like sheep to help us sleepwork, hush
those numbers,
and what kind of quiet would there be? and
in that quiet what would it mean to be free,?
to be heard,?
would that be the real beginning of the word?; 'words...'
words, and the words would be, ours,
and our words would be the only bonds,

stories of gods or faith, which came first?,
the water or the thirst?,
well we are sort of 90 percent water,
so our thirst is water and our water is thirst,
and we are all, all human, so...
we, the 99 percent
can overcome this money as the innocent,? And
quench each others thirst,.
And these money bonds burst!
These money wands, break, for
our children and our children's children's sake,
can we let money decide for itself what it is or isn't worth, then
something that has no inherent worth
could cost the earth,

Have the banks and their governments got our sanity,
under lock and key, while this forgery,
passes itself off as humanity?
Lets unhinge money's doors, the time has passed to pause,
to sit behind locked doors sucking through last straws,
Let us organise, rise, break and recreate money's laws,

part 3

Money is as innocent as the gun
an inverting reflection from the deification of the sun,
this innocence,
it can not feel the difference,
on a cheek, between a first and a last breath,
so to speak,

Money is as innocent as the gun,
a reinccurring abstraction,
bringing every thing under one,
this innocence,
it can not see the difference, between how children thrive,
and how they just stay alive,

Money is as innocent as the gun,
a reoccurring insinuation of who to sacrifice begun,
this innocence,
it can't tell the difference,
between an extracted tortured scream,
and the expression of a finally fulfilled dream,

Money is as innocent as the gun,
an adhering predation, so for to worship a one,
this innocence, it can not hear the difference,
between a first word spoke,
and a last farewell unvoiced choke,

Money is as innocent as the gun,
a reassuring restoration of the silence in fun,
this innocence,
it can not be, the difference,
between yes, and no,

Money is as innocent as the gun,
an averting reflection between our stories told and spun,
this innocence it can not tell the difference,
between a crowded beach of sun tan lotioned ice cream eaters being bugged by flies,
and the exhumed mass grave of fly swarmed eyes,

Money is as innocent as the gun.

MONEY IS
AS
INNOCENT
AS
THE SUN

Debt

money is as innocent as the sun,
but as debts, to pay which one?,
a catch 22 like situation of remuneration,
the repayment of one, money, is the other's collection,
at a 'disinterest rate' of burgeoning catastrophic extortion,
that will have us bound and...
sorry; that will have them, bound and gagged,
dumped on a beach, wearing concrete shoes,
shoes of concrete abstraction,
their muffled cries of Canute-commands,
falling on the deaf ears of a sea,
which we,
have leveraged to become an ocean,
maybe this is going to be the resolution,
of that walking contradiction,

the species for whom, being, is a life or death situation,
my preference is for a slow death; about, this speed,...
'bum bum, maybe a bit slower, ***'bum   bum,'***,
Life, is Good!,... and then there's .. ***living***!, bum bum, **bum bum, bum bum,**
living a temporary state of togetherness,
death a permanent state of separation,
this is more than enough of a ridiculous situation,
with out us putting up with living being misshapen,
as some kind of repayment scheme for money's accumulation, ,
what is this... a life for death situation!?,
life; a credit to being, mm? Mm? Yes,
but surely not to be repaid in the living,
life a given, which has been misshapen,
in this accumulating misappropriation,
of the commonfold,
in the midst of life, we are in the midst of money, sold,
as it's numbers unfold,
the qualities of life as a subordinate conjunction,
to the loneliest consumption, death,
death, between you and me, money, as a given,
beyond giving, or receiving,
a stick thrown for us to spend a life time retrieving,
a price on your head for not believing,
a blasphemy for which it'll cut off your body,
and leave you dreaming, on the street,

I repeat, life a given, which money has... 'ssh'
'less of the feck-cund abstraction', I here you say,
'careful, consider the market's reaction,'
life, a derivative collateralised excavation,
lives debts, in-securitised, for collection,
no prizes for guessing which ones,
this innocence, the appearance, that the difference, in skin it can not tell,
as it peels it, in the cell, sell, sell, sell, sell,
rise from your money alibis,
money alibis like a bell, done!, done!, done,

salivating in the sea, its like... salivating in the sea, salivating in the sea...

Light

money is as innocent as the sun,
both loosing their shine to this pollution,
for history, come fistory,
of mother nature by her youngest son,
while holding the gun,
to a saturation point, we are market stricken,
a headless chicken,
money did anoint,
to the point, of no return?,
tipping tipping tipping as we burn,
to distraction, this carbon extraction,
for money's accumulation,
drought nation after drought nation,
hungry for rivers down which they've been sold,
this reoccurring privatising dispossession of the commonfold,

fold!, money please!,
put your cards on the table and walk,
this gamble was just a fable, cheap talk,
of weather incidence, by and buy and buy and buy and by coincidence,
untold, light's silence, the silence of light,
the clickless trigger of time's finishing gun,
light, oh light, what have we done?,
this innocence, all the graceful elegance,
of the later stages of malnutrition,

The agitation of sacrifice

Sacrifices' agitation...
water wishes water like 'dust to dust',
the sun has got his hat on for the... er!, is it made of the earth's crust,

money,
the conspiracy,
that has us believing,

we are the theory,
not to be believed,
our credibility relieved,
of it's duty,
to make believe our truth is beauty,
not just to be seen to behold,
but to be cherished in the commonfold,

have we been dangling so long on the end of this line that we've been sold,
that, "there is no such thing as the commonfold",
that we can no longer be bold,
now that life is the penalty,
if life is a penalty are we really dying or just living?
and if living is given and if giving is receiving,
can we make truth and stop believing, money the conspiracy?,

money, a performance enhancing substance,
taken, as our absence,
that's puts us in our place,
in the closing stages of our race,
and it must have felt so much like it had all just begun,
after the last world peace was won,

never again,
never again for money to reign,
in the absolute,
with the power to mute,
to degrade, to starve into submission,
decency, humanity and dignity,
for the sake of money's silent partner capitalist fascism,

money,
the conspirici,

ok, i know that's not quite correct but it does rhyme with alibi,
it wasn't you, nor me, how could it be we,

and surely not I,
we're the species of the alibi,
from totemic mitigation,

through prophetic inspiration,

to money's circulation,
it wasn't you, or me, how could it be we, and surely not I,

money's absence is our presence,
our fortuity, money's necessity,
money's certainty, our confusion,
our doubt, money's foregone conclusion,

money,
the conspiracy,
an abstract surrogacy,
the mother we never had?
Well, nature never wanted us, not really,
and she is a bit touchy feely, joke!,

money, the conspiracy,
the final frontier of theories, not to be believed,
I dare you,
I will if you will,
can it be as difficult as it seems?,

for a species self-domesticating through our shared waking dreams,
where shadows cast figures and smoke with out fire fuels our schemes,
money a conspiracy?
as theories go, I've heard worse,
would you believe me if I told you it was the premise of a prize winning verse?,
first prize a publishing deal,
some financial security at last; how does that feel?,
I got the contract in the post the other day,
I don't know how many times I read it,

I thought I might bringing it here to read to you today,
but I didn't, no, I tore it up, and I threw it away,

Why? ..
Well, I'd like to say, it was a matter of conscience and consistency,
not having those words possessed by money's conspiracy,
but, if I told you that I would be fibbing,

cos what it was was, this prize winning verse was full of metaphors,
of keeping the wolf from these doors,
and this contract had a clause,
a metaphors clause, if any metaphors, turn out to be fact,

end of contract,
and how was I suppose to know,
that some... 'well what year is it?... say 2020... well,

some forty one years ago,
the wolf had been re-introduced to these shores,

talk about a last straws!,
yes, I am up for that,
but I really think we should stop sucking through them any more...
I thought, if I could find out who was to blame,

for the reintroduction of the wolf to these shores,

there might be a loss of earnings claim,
I visited the offices of one of those firms you see, advertised on TV,
no win no fee... office!?
It was a facade,
a familiar looking gentlemen came in,

he had the air of the Marque de Sade,
but he wasn't... phew!... he gave me his card,
Mr. S, Holmes, Sherlock!?

He gestured, he offered, he tied me to a chair,
and started talking to me, as you'd expect,

like I wasn't quite 'all there',

but looking deep into my eyes with this imperious entitled werewolf like stare,
and talking in a voice that didn't sound like him,
and I'm not just saying that cos I can't do the impersonation,
"you've got that cockamamie, everyone's against me,

self flagellating theory look in your eyes,"
have I? have I?
"all conspiracies and lies,

oh spare me the whys, and the wherefores,
the wolf, re-introduced to these shores,

oh sure!, let me guess, to replace those three lions with something indigenous on all fours,

with teeth and fur, but not claws,
wolves don't have claws!", wolves don't have claws!",

wolves don't have claws!",
But, I said, with a certain amount of trepidation, like lions, wolves do have paws,...
... No, not pause... paws,
He gestured for me to hand him my mobile, I did,

he put my mobile and his mobile into a sound proof box,
his voice and his whole demeanor changed,
he said;
"I'm so awfully sorry to come across like some self hating Zionist,
Werewolf, Israeli Apartheidist,
I'm not like that in the least,

it's a BBC-friendly pretense,
I'm having to maintain in case of any surveillance",
surveillance?...

he said, I might have a claim, really!
the wolf was re-introduced to these shores, yes, but not literally,
it was an attempt,

by the establishment,

all those years ago,

to reduce the figures of poverty on these islands to an all time low,

figuratively,
the wolf wasn't actually,
released into public parks, housing estates or the urban wild,
no, such places a lone parent or carer would always accompany a child;

and the poor?
well, the wolf you see,
can't be relied upon in the reduction of adult poverty,
the prowess of the wolf is somewhat fabled,
unless that adult was alone, weak with hunger and/or disabled,

and stories spread of impoverished parents carrying out acts of
selfless heroism,
that can't be allowed can it, that might create some kind of moral
ideological prism,
the poor shown in such a light,
it might, insightful fill,

minds awash in newspaper ink swill,
and who knows what such insight might instill,

it might placing in jeopardy,
this 'unwritten policy',
vis a vis,

a chord might be struck,
that resonates back to that stand that we took,
alone, when European fascism was gaining currency,
alone we faced invasion, ruin and bankruptcy,

a people not too big to fail?,
no financial institutions,

forth coming with rescue packages solutions, for to bail?,
its hard to say,

its going to be difficult to hear,

but it would appear...

that it was neither here .. nor there...

to this money, if we did or didn't prevail,

but prevail we did,
and the dollar accrued enough leverage to screw down tight that lid,
on the old world empires of racial persecution and supremacy,
with a post war policy,
of, 'dictatorships for democracy', when it suited,

and with peace at last,
came a loss of patience on mass,
with money's license to pass off, Them as Us,

and Us as Them, until 'peace at last'...
recast, the shadow of that incredulous class,
'pardon, 'the common good'?!, isn't that a oxymoron'?

and with peace at last came a loss of patience on mass,
with money's license to pass, off,
peace as war,
and war as peace,
still a binding lease,
with so many prices to pay,
just one that gives the right to say,

'a people's war begets a people's peace?',
loud and proud,
that phrase can be heard,
in those two minutes without a word,
at the annual memory letting stone,
two minute silence down-loadable as a ring tone,...
... 'excuse me!', I think we should answering that?

Cause if sacrifice is,
money's antithesis,
beyond measures praxis,
then sacrifice is the axis,

on which our story turns,
our actions spurns,
alibi's reflections,
to follow dignity's directions,

so the wolf... so the wolf made itself scarce in lairs off shore,
salivating for money's more, money's more money's more...

tides not yet rising though,

for money's more, money's more...
across the pond waited,
breath baited,

laid in wait,
for that sense of war time predation,
to abate,
and the wolf laid in wait,
and the wolf laid in wait,
for a generation to translate,
sacrifice through pomp and ceremony's bait,

'Comrades in arms',
in the mouths of our leaders,
minus the munitions,
that expression quickly begins to lose its charms,

'Comrades in arms',
they relish that phrase, and how it embalms,

heroism's inflamed cooperation,
as war, just as war, as nation, just as nation,

pitter patter, pitter patter...

those sacrifices made, did they have a half life of thirty odd years, to then begin to fade,
in to a back ground sound,
only to be heard,
in those two minutes without a...,
pitter patter pitter patter, pitter patter echoed those paws,
through the banks, the courts, the government's, the orphanages' corridors,

I heard the Royal prerogative was used,
to get around those draconian child protection rules,
and wolves were released into schools,
not all schools of course,
that might lead to a spate of divorce,
amongst certain MPs,
they can deal with that exemption being used to increase school fees,
cause what is money for,

if not to keep the wolf from money's door,

pitter patter...

a half life of thirty odd years?!

let's remember, to forget...
let's remember, to let, go...
yeah!... maybe it was all just a guileless collective loss of memory?

of course, no unwritten policy,

... the secret services infiltrating trade unions and government ministry,

to destablise a growing socialised economy,

oh dearie dearie,

a conspiracy? the establishment involved in secrecy,

they were most probably, just weary,
of their media chums mocking by-lines and sniggers,
'wolves?' wolves?',

nothing sinister, like avoiding coming on TV to make denials like,

"These wolves are merely nursery rhyme figures"

I don't recall, when I was a young man, any stories on the local or national news,
of wolves disembarking, with expressions on their faces like they've got nothing to lose,
seeking out the vulnerable; while wondering up and down our beaches,
that hasn't happened, that couldn't happen...

cause we would fight them on them wouldn't we, so history teaches,

in those iconic speeches,
with layer upon layer of that plural possessive adjective,
that reaches,
to create a sense of commonality, whose?
that beseeches,
time to be a reality,
possessed of a self-possessing power,
our, time; as if time was rebooted,
for those for whom it had previously suited,
time to be instituted, in its passing,
solely in the amassing of fortunes accrued from
the exploited, pillaged and looted,

money made, in the shade,

of the empires parade,

handing out flags poised...,
"And it's a lovely sunny afternoon, and the people are out on the streets,

flags poised to wave,

first comes, the shallow grave,
followed closely by the sounds of the mass grave,

oh, and there's the regal, wave?,
for the fly swarm past in close formation,
of early grave, after early grave, after early grave,

after early grave, after early grave, after early grave...

a heart warming wave,

for the unmarked grave,

forever there, somewhere,
a tumultuous cheer,

from those taking up the rear,

the pauper's grave,
eyes to the right for money's crusade,
that converts to degrade, life to dig its own,

under the imperial serial searing never setting sun",

suddenly!, that time became one...
our time...
Our finest hour... so far?

... are we still taking of breaths which were given,
that we might not be,
enwaged as the property of that tyranny?,
or is that no longer physically a possibility?
Has this air, since those sacrifices, been replenished, cleansed
completely,
of that consensus-sensuality, of air,
that once filled this lung with the commonality,

a duty of care,
for the generations to come, not to bare,

not to be,
enwaged, at the mercy,

of the tyranny, of property,

sacrifices agitation,

to regenerate the social obligation,

to agitate, to reinstate, to rejuvenate property,

to be a party, to the commonfold,

not to be sold,

the agitation of sacrifice; does there always
have to be such a terrible price, paid,

before the beauty of promise,

a promise of such beauty can be made, and kept?,

to obligate, to agitate, to agitate to obligate,

to generate a generation,

to create this never again land, isn't that the sea?, steady!,

dare we, give agency, to our imagination,

at the risk of invoking the disquieting obligation,

to take action, on behalf of the coming generation,

with a generosity of spirit,

that can take you beyond the limit,

of con-formity, dare we? Steady!,

let's remember .. to forget,
let's remember .. to let,

go of now,
that difficult time,
we're not ready to face, not yet;
not now!,
let's remember how,
If sacrifice is,
money's antithesis,
beyond measures praxis,
so sacrifice is the axis,
on which our story turns,
a generation learns, and forgets,
learns and lets, go
of now,
that difficult time,
we're not ready to face,
not yet;
not now!,

let's remember how, it was,
when it like wasn't now,...
... yes!... oh.. just me then,...
when it wasn't a time of regret,
remembering wasn't done to forget,
it was how the present and the future met,
in a resonance, of remembrance beyond ceremony,
shared losses antidote to peace and wars alchemy,

let's remember,
to breath in, to breath out, to breath in, to share,
our breath was... is the air,
but not the other way around,
or we'd be in trouble, serious trouble,
we are,
again, money does reign, in the absolute,

with a power and prerogative to loot,
and to riot,

through our communities, our water, our food,
our homes, our air, on the quiet,

rampaging on the QT,
havocking money's insecurity,

into the lonely family,
smashed and grabbed,

youthful suicide slabbed,

polluting is not like looting,
our children's children's future,
in no way does it resemble a riot,

it is comparatively quiet,
lets go dancing in the streets and defy it,

money, the conspiracy,
that has us believing that we are the theory,
not to be believed,
our credibility deceived,
of it's duty,
to make believe our truth is beauty,
not just to be seen to be sold,
but to be cherished... lets enfold, them
and wrap them up in swaddling adorned with flowers from wreaths,
red and black,
don't let them see the courage that we lack,
and lay them down by the annual memory letting stone,
and whisper lullabies, lullabies of the unknown known,
we're not just going to be pictured memories on a phone,
their pride in what you are doing for them,

will carry you with them, into the unknown known,

‘there there, there there now...

there there, there there now,’

and they’ll remember to forget,

they’ll remember to let go of now,
that time we couldn’t face, not yet,

not... ‘there there there their now,

their now is now...’

Trespass

We have made visual contact and are now approaching the object,

It's a gigantic dismembered finger, toward the surface of the water, pointed,

No, correction, It's an elongated,

sea-salted, pock riddled stone,

symbols, a language,

a memorial reminding the tide to atone?

Tides turn, tides just turn,

words, a phrase,

Le t'$ we forg et?

Le t'$ we forget?

Le t's we forget, let's we forget,

Who or whatever they were, their past appears to have been met,

The Confidence Stick

money, is as innocent as the sun,

the first and maybe the final con-fusion,

the equivalence of light, oh? Oh!, the majesty!,

the 'big regal we, I am'

promise to pay, sovereignty, sham,

all that glittering light,

without an atom of truth in sight, to see,

usurped by this, 'promise to what?!', banking dynasty,

the 'House of Money', lair,

with its private/public money made out of thin air,

whose thin air?, our thin air!, whose thin air?, our thin air!, whose thin air?, our thin air!,

the 'House of Money',

to which we owe such a debt of loyalty,

the loyalty of debt,

the default to which this banking money privatised is set,

in digitalised, stone,

the education, the car, the wedding, the holiday, the operation,
the home loan,

debt as security?, whose?

if the credit card and the mortgage,

had been the rage,

before 1833,

they might not have abolished slavery,

they might have expanded it on the grounds of discrimination,

to include 99 percent of the nation,

now subjects of this privatised, monetised, sovereignty,

subjects bereft of a citizens currency,

subjects subjected to this birth-written oath of liquidity,

I swear as a faithful commodity,

not to share,

nor to lead a life of mutually beneficial co-operation, and creative solidarity,

but to wear these link-less chains of singularity,

shackled to the lonely family,

and this I swear by the almighty,

trinity, of money making money, money,

the boundary,

between you, me, between the 'I and the am',

'I borrow, therefore, I swallow, circulated like money's Spam,

spun atoms, whirling in berserker like insecurity,

our threads of sociality,

torn cut unspun,

for the respin,

of win, win, you've got to win,

so they can loose,

check your phone, cos your alone,

panic to choose,

you've got to win so they can loose,

you've got to win,

shopping din, selling grin,

just put it in the bin,

spendin grin, just put it in the bin,

the spending sham, the big therefore I am!'

money spending like a veil,

the 'I am', shame-faced,

the 'I am' so alone, when for sale,

paying off your life's witness to testify,

I swear to spend the truth,

the whole truth and nothing but the truth, so help me,

help me money,

spending money like an alibi,

I can positively identify,

it wasn't me,

I was here, in this country,

check my credit card record, there, you see,

this innocence,

a more than unhappy coincidence,

in increments,

of less than a dollar a day,

bargains taking breaths, breaths taken, in bite size payments to hide,

if you are what you eat,

what if you repeatedly swallow your pride?,

a Stockholm syndrome epidemic, world wide?,

this is a hostage situation you do need to take a side,

"excuse me, erm, sorry to interrupt,"

'Yes'

"You may not have notice but my seat was reserved, I am not with these, people... so if you required any assistance; tying anyone up, foreclosing mortgages, sanctioning benefits, making people redundant, or just persuading these people that there's nothing to be done... VIP triple A list .. "

money, is as innocent as the sun,

a meteoric collision,

of the concrete and abstraction,

beneath its plume of star dust calculating accumulating
percentaged refraction,

in its glaring shade, qualities function,

this dark age like dissolution, of worth,

begs the question, is this, our world of this earth,

the last refuge of money, and religion coincidently,

is the same prism, through which to cleanse the eye of humanity,

in a purity, of unadulterated nullity,

in which the world is a stage, a phase,

in profit and prophecy,

and we're not here, not literally,

this innocence, life's equivalence,

excelsis-in-extinctions, excelsior-in-abstraction,

The Estate of Money

money, is as innocent as the sun,

the money estate borderless, the estate of money, without horizon,

rising as the nation, setting as the gun,

that from which, without their lives, so many run,

an empire of extraction,

for expansion, expansion for extraction,

an empire, with a vampire, like reflection, uh!, non,

well, one,

to be seen in the eyes of those who have run,

a gift, a conversion,

humanity to civilisation, civilisation to humanity,

an opportunity,

knocking on our doors,

to see, to hear, to feel, to think,

to pause,

to pause the calamity of money's laws,

a currency that can not fund wars,

humanity,

it does not wash up on shores,

it debases this sham sovereignty,

of bank corruption-cy,

that put the mock in de-moc-racy,

the bogus refugee, a byline in history,

the headline; 'a world wide fake identity, scam revealed',

'nationality',

in which eyes, ears, hearts, minds, and lips are sealed,

rubber stamped and congealed,

in blood untold,

this earth one foreign field,

forever exhumed of its Midas yield,

sold,

and sold, and sold and...

until we embolden,

wield worth, weaved with this earth,

by the quality of commonality,

that beseeches time to teach us humility,

to be dispossessed of that money vanity contest,

of more, more to the power of more, more than the rest,

rest...

let us rest from this incessant insistence,

that we are contestants,

in a race against time, as money,

it can be rebooted, as trans-nationality,

and instituted, in a solidarity,

to occupy the money estate,

and to liberate sovereignty,

from the banks,

from that, and any majesty,

that demeans commonality,

and from money, as the state of the nation,

a money state, a state of abstract occupation,

in which its collaborators with their amoral sophistication,

claim the benefits of environmental degradation,

their impersonation, of border guards, done unconvincingly,

show me your papers, oh, sir, madam, all that paperless paper,

that will do very nicely,

would you like these people to recount their woes,

while those people to touch their toes,

a selection of lubricants, blood, sweat, fears...

as of yet though,

relatively few, so,

far have run,

from the cradles of civilisation,

to the cradles of abstraction,

where money won,

the competition, of unintended consequences,

and begun,

the slow burning,

sacrifices, to the sun,

that from which so many will run,

money, more ran from than to, to you, to me,

a humanitarian emergency, UN declared,

resolution prepared,

passed,

a license to print money,

millions, billions, to support, and to... welcome... every refugee,

hold on, hold on!, that's an import, and export license,

for weapons and their not so safe delivery,

money, the price to meet,

I repeat, life a given,

which money has..., which money has,

this money is like your death,

it's yours, but it can't belong to you,

money like life, can't be yours,

but, it does belong to you,

this innocence, our presence as absence, to
be, to long, to share to belong,

Extortion

salivating .. in the sea...just, salivating .. in the sea...

money is as innocent as the sun,

light given appearance, taken as a reflection,

for the of equivalence, one,

money, paying for the disappearance of worth,

the abduction of that incommensurable throng,

the qualities of life's song, sung,

and the ransom demand, that we keep stum,

that we keep our selves to ourselves, that we play dumb,"

"we know you're in there, we have the bank surrounded,

release the hostage unharmed, and you can go free,"

'what!?, money roaming the streets of our community, free,

steady!,'

at no point in our history,

has there been such a urgency,

for worth, to be returned to our hands,

but how on earth, are we meant to agree, to these demands,

a catch 22 like kidnap negotiation,

when the ransom is the hostage and the hostage is the ransom,

because worth is our intelligence, our togetherness,

belonging, our expression,

the more than the parts of any sum,

any sum of money deal,

any sum of money that can congeal,

into prices with a compulsion to steal,

to feed money's habit,

cos money's gotta to have it,

money's gotta have it so fucking bad its unreal,

prices steal,

each mouthful of a parents denied skipped meal,

'I ate something earlier,'

'Where's your plate?,' '

Don't be cheeky'

prices steal, light,

by which to learn to write, to learn to re ..,

'Oh no, does that mean we have to go to bed now?'

prices steal, food, seed by seed,

a systematic kleptomania, disembodied greed,
the price of money; "the best money, tremendous
money, fabulous money, money for ever, money for
real..."
more so it would appear than our response ability is to
maintain this homes earthly feel,

degree by degree, money so real,

price as consequence,

in the head lights of the present tense,

frozen,
in a token, casting a shadow puppet adherence,

a kin to the cave wall experience,

the Platonic one,

a forlorn abstraction,

prices just a reaction,

to the reaction of prices... reaction!,

reactionary money,

the price is, what ever suffices, boom or crisis,

it suffices, prices without consciences, justifications pricked,

by obligations, that contradict,

those measures being taken,

as those precious given treasures are being forsaken,

for money, to be made, 'made money',

with a Cosa Nostra like code of silence,

to conceal,

the everyday depleting polluting, dirty violence,

exacted,

for our consuming compliance,

to feel, relieved, by numbers, a bu..., a bu...,

a bulimic like urge that overcomes us,

to converge, in the loneliest of numbers,

appearance money, 'mine!'...

money appearance,

appearance by the light of money,

prices,

in which life is,

an expendable spendable sum,

in this money power, power money conundrum,

no one is owed a life,

if no one's owed a living,

lives are debts and debts are lives for collection,

our epochal deception,

a tale, sold by idiot numbers, empty of sound and fury,

signifying everything,

everything under the sun,

going going going...

neither with a bang nor a whimper,

but a peel, of bells rung,

to call back our pasts to kneel among,

and to wish, and to wish, and to wish that it was real,

this carbon fundamentalist denial,

this capitalist zeal,

degree by degree, the earth is loosing,

the earth is loosing its homely feel,,

in this innocence, with all the spinning confidence,

of a blindfolded auction,

'could you please join me in putting on your blindfolds?,

unless of course your afraid of the dark of course, then just close your eyes, this is a once in a life time opportunity, to be the owner of this life of... opportunity,... this priceless time of opportunity of... this time of time, this life time... time of life... opportunity time of... opportunity... this... with a reserve price of money ...do I hear more? More?, more going once, more going twice, going, going, going, going, gone...

sold for less, to 'extinction plc, corporation',

Enhanced interrogation method

An odious sound like smell, breaking the surface of the water,

bloating niece, floating cousins, sister?,

grasping mother, clasping daughter,

in water, wishing water, like dust to dust,

water pulled wish bones, like the glimmer to hope,

between the jolt and the judder at the end of a rope,

the fingers entwined, are holding,

love defying water heaving, water so heavy so heavy with its obligation,

to do the bidding of the sun,

sacrifices to our star,

not just those cut throat temples,

life's blood flowing like a spar,

or those to be commemorated, those

generations to come,

no, no our sacrifices to that star, have begun,

their great unfolding,

but these hands, these hands are holding,

the fingers are entwined, though not accompanying a prayer,

no, they haven't got one, but, both below to a different pair,

of which the smaller hand,

like a last breath that will not be taken,

is holding closed that curtain,

mud churned, behind which her short life is passing,

Cradled by arms,

that are lost in the charms, of a life,

held through those long fretful nights of ridiculous assurances sought,

that the sleep of the innocent is naught,

more nor less than sleep,

to be someone's to keep,

supported balancing on one tip toe, ankle deep,

in bubble bath,

'if you don't hold my hand, we'll never get across this road and we'll
miss the bus, the party won't wait for you to start',

what a face, little noses were made for bubble bath?,

as a dog pulling on its lead comes on to the path,

in the shade of that precaution,

taken,

held, maybe there's a sense held,

held in the chill of that shade,

a sense of those wishes not made,

of thought, bones snagged caught,

in a mind being torn to pieces by hope, distraught,

hooded by water that small face to distort,

the holding in these hands a refusal to divulge,

in a deluge, of water, water pouring like torture,

like torture, consigned, to a blind, spot,

just a piece of mind, tied, a forget me knot,

tied, for the peace of mind of the haves and the have got,

that's us lot,

so, when waiting to cross a busy road, do take care,

in that vigilance,

there maybe a semblance, there,

of that between you, that small hand you hold,

and those fingers entwined, as old,

and as blind as love, older,

uncannily bolder,

the terror pulled wish bones,

in water wishing water like dust to dust,

the sun has got his hat on for the parade of the returning,

from our burning, to the earth's trust,

held by love, yes, these hands are held by love,

but, it is the hands that are holding,

with love defying, you, me, this every no one,

fit for purpose terror blind, mist, capitalist, jamboree,

this not me, this just me,

the hands... the fingers, and the contumacious love; parting,

not letting go, no, but not holding,

like autumn leaves in winter puddles these fingers are unfolding,

fingers are...

Day light Larceny

money is as innocent as the sun,

as an accumulating fusion,

it melts,

the mercies, of shared experience,

the duties, to life's inheritance,

and casts them in a mold, the shape of things undone,

and puts it against your head like a gun,

money's will spiraling, persuasions,

of such hypnotic, despotic, abstracting, sensations,

feel that cold comforting, ring,

money's will spiraling, nothings,

it's siren sings,

that nothing, at the end of a gun,

that, 'there's nothings to see here, understand!

the finger on the trigger belongs to the invisible hand,

has some one been making money in the bank of this Eng-land?,

when the lights aren't on,

don't even try and answer that question,

your feeling so drowsy, so busy, so browsey,

there's no need of a reality,

money's will, will be,

day light robbery,

the robbery of day light,

which is plunging us into this twilight,

of the obligations,

to those generations, to come,

money's will, will be done, understand,

some one has been making money, in the Bank of this land,

and they've left a note,

it looks like it's been written by your hand,

an IOU forged, a UOI?,

a debt to ourselves,

surely, that's not something we would buy,

that would be like,

taking the stand to testify,

on behalf of the person who picked your pocket, as their alibi,

'yes, they were standing next to me at that time',

and the jury found guilty, facing a sentence,

for reaching a verdict using their reason and conscience,

instead of just tossing a coin,

it would be like, the Bank of this-whose-land?,

instructed by governments,

to create 'public financial instruments',

'People's shares', for want of a better phrase,

and them being sold on the financial markets to raise,

money that pays, off the debts,

of private commercial banking, for want of a better phrase,

and these 'People's shares', with which the option to redeem,

blames lives, claims lives, through money's benefit scheme,

Qualitative Easing,

squeezing, qualities from lives; that then have to be lived,

sieved, through vicarious, self esteem,

precarious, in the single syllable selfie celeb dream, of me, me, me ..,

sieved through the pain of loneliness, the loneliness of pain,

with its struggle to sustain,

a sense of self regarding presence,

Qualitative Easing, seizing assets,

needed to begin and to end a day,

I know I shouldn't really ask, but could you stay,

a bit longer today?

anguish masked like a blocked drain,

'Sorry, I've got to get to my next client...'

time passing like a missed train,

you could make yourself a cup of tea, 'Sorry',

the disdain of money, making money, financing finance,

the riotous stasis,

of this is, how it is, and always will be,

austerity trance, the same old same,

money's resistance, by any other name,

poll taxing, poleaxing, the disabled, the poor, the vulnerable,

the young,

from day to day, strung out strung up to pay,

money's debts behind and before our very eyes,

wide shut with an incredulity, that denies,

money's will, does not have to be done,

on earth as if this is some kind of eternity spun,

speculation, for accumulation, incineration, for consumption,

for GDP, to infinity,

this innocence, it does not convince,

so let it be said,

pull the fucking trigger money, go on,

cause if this is some kind of eternity then we're already dead,

salivating in the sea!, its like, salivating in the sea, salty?
No those are the tears that belong to you, me,

Straining to Ring

money is as innocent as the sun,

when all is said and unspun,

in essence, an indifference, of a gun,

this power money, money power con-nun-numbdrum,

an ındifference to an inheritance undone,

though, is it wise,

to relying on the desserts and the seas to rise,

with all the righteous wroth of an ocean,

as the resistance,

to this desolating dictatorship of accumulation?,

their means and ends calibration,

also take nothing into consideration,

least of all the dispossessed sub-primed person,

maybe, this innocence,

it hasn't, cause it can't eclipse,

our other sun,

our conscience shared in motion,

proletarian fusion, our power to over come,

to not keep ourselves to our selves ,

or to be kept stum,

to rise, to revolutionise,

to unbind ties, of spinning alibis,

not to play dumb,

but to be embraced by the wisdom,

of this earth,

where birth, was given love,

and love was given birth,

for what it's worth,

for what it is, worth,

between you and me, worth, it's not between you, me,

its between you, me,

there is no price to meet, no equivalence you see,

can you feel those, can you hear those chimes of possibility,

the spring coiled in History, to become Ourstory,

this quality, of commonality,

is straining, to ring,

from every place of work, healing, leisure, learning,

without it there's just this slow burning,

denied compliance,

in which quickly,

we need to find in each others hearts, quickly,

the courage of defiance,

rise, organise, resist with a love that creates as it defies,

capitalism's reduction,

capitalism abduction,

its depleting competing ablution,

rise, to be realised by ties of worth,

cause maybe as a life,

we have not yet discovered our selves on this planet,

still called earth, come on, for what it is worth, come on.

www.ingramcontent.com/pod-product-compliance
Lightning Source LLC
Chambersburg PA
CBHW060611310726
48982CB00003B/522

* 9 7 8 1 7 3 9 2 3 2 5 0 4 *